LUCY DA

The Playful Puppy

Hodder
Children's
Books

A division of Hachette Children's Books

To Sophie and Benjamin –
two Cairn terriers, who were the best little pals
in the world

Special thanks to Narinder Dhami

Little Animal Ark is a trademark of Working Partners Limited
Text copyright © 2001 Working Partners Limited
Created by Working Partners Limited, London, W6 0QT
Illustrations copyright © 2001 Andy Ellis

First published in Great Britain in 2001 by Hodder Children's Books

This edition published in 2007

The rights of Lucy Daniels and Andy Ellis to be identified as the author
and illustrator of this work respectively have been asserted by them in
accordance with the Copyright, Designs and Patents Act 1988.

1

A Catalogue record for this book is available from the
British Library

ISBN-13: 978 0 340 93250 6

Printed and bound in Great Britain by Clays Ltd, St Ives plc

Hodder Children's Books
A division of Hachette Children's Books
338 Euston Road, London NW1 3BH

Chapter One

"I'm going to the Juniors!" Mandy Hope sang as she clattered down the stairs.

"Breakfast first, Mandy," said her mum, Emily Hope, smiling. "You've got a busy day ahead of you."

It was the first day of term. Mandy had been longing for today to arrive. She was moving up from the Infants to the Juniors!

But there was another reason for being excited . . .

Her friend Peter Foster had collected his new Cairn terrier puppy last night. And Peter had said that he and his mum would be bringing the puppy to school with them this morning!

Mandy loved animals, which was a good thing, as there was always lots of them at home!

Her mum and dad were vets. Their surgery, Animal Ark, was at the back of their house, in the village of Welford.

Mandy didn't have any pets of her own, though. Animal Ark was busy enough! But her friends' pets were the next best thing.

Adam Hope, Mandy's dad, came into the kitchen. He laughed as Mandy tried to eat her cornflakes as fast as she could.

"Slow down, there's plenty of time," he said. "I'm taking you to school today. Mum's on Animal Ark duty."

Mrs Hope pulled on her white coat and gave Mandy a quick hug. "Have a good day, love," she said. "See you later." Then she hurried into the Animal Ark surgery.

Mandy got up and put her empty bowl in the sink. "Finished! Can we go now, please, Dad?"

Mandy could hardly sit still as her father drove through Welford.

She was surprised when her dad stopped the Land-rover outside the Infants gate at Welford Village School. "What are you doing, Dad?" she asked. "I'm not in the Infants any more

– I'm in the Juniors, now!"

"I'm sorry, Mandy," said Mr Hope. "I nearly forgot." Then he winked at her.

"Oh, *Dad!*" Mandy laughed.

Mr Hope drove a bit further on, to the Juniors gate.

Mandy looked through the railings at the big Junior playground. She was excited, but a bit scared, too.

She soon cheered up though, when she saw Peter and Mrs Foster at the school gate. Peter was holding a tiny bundle of sandy-coloured fur in his arms.

"Look, Dad," Mandy said breathlessly. "There's Peter's new puppy!"

She climbed out of the car, and rushed over.

"Hi, Mandy!" Peter called. He smiled widely as he spotted his friend. "Come and say hello to Timmy!"

The puppy looked up at Mandy with dark, shining eyes. He gave a little woof and wagged his short stumpy tail.

Mandy thought Timmy was *lovely.* He was small but sturdy, and his fluffy coat was a sandy colour, except for dark smudges on his face. And he had sweet ears that flopped over at the corners.

"Hello, Timmy," Mandy said. She gently stroked the puppy's head. Timmy sniffed her hand, and then licked it with his little pink tongue. "Oh, Peter, he's so cute!"

"He certainly is," agreed Mr Hope, after he had parked the car and followed Mandy over. "Hello, boy!"

Peter grinned proudly. "Do

you want to hold him, Mandy?"
he asked.

"Oh, can I?" Mandy gasped.

Peter handed Timmy over.
The puppy didn't seem to mind,
and he cuddled down happily in
Mandy's arms.

She held him carefully, loving the
feel of Timmy's solid, warm body.

As Mandy rubbed her cheek against his soft fur, Timmy sniffed her ear, then gave her a big, wet lick on the nose.

"Did you take him for a walk this morning, Peter?" Mandy asked.

"No, Timmy's only eight weeks old," Peter said. "He has to have more injections before he's allowed to walk around outside. Until then, we have to carry him everywhere."

Mr Hope nodded. "Timmy will come to Animal Ark for his injections in four weeks' time, Mandy," he said. "You know why they are so important, don't you?"

Mandy nodded. "They will help stop Timmy catching illnesses from outside," she said.

"That's right," her dad agreed. "After his injections, Timmy will be able to go for walks quite safely."

"Mum, can Mandy come round to our house after school?" Peter asked.

"Yes, of course, if Mr Hope agrees," Mrs Foster said, smiling.

"Can I, please, Dad?" Mandy asked eagerly.

"Of course you can, love," Mr Hope told her. "There's the bell. Off you go, now."

Mandy gave Timmy a last cuddle, and handed him over to Peter's mum. Then she followed Peter into the big Juniors playground.

Chapter Two

Mandy opened her new writing book at the first page. Her first day in Class 3 had been fun, so far. Mandy was on the same table as Peter, which was great! And their new teacher, Miss Rushton, seemed very friendly.

"Put the date at the top of the page, please," Miss Rushton told them. "Now I want to hear all about what you did in the holidays. And I want to see some nice pictures too," she added.

Mandy thought for a while, and then decided to write about the day her gran and grandad took her to the seaside. As she picked up her pencil, she glanced across at Peter. He'd already started writing. Mandy leaned over to read it.

I got my new puppy, Timmy, last night. He's a Cairn terrier, and he's great. I played with him for a bit. Then he went to sleep. Mum says puppies need to rest a lot, but I hope Timmy doesn't sleep <u>all</u> the time!

Peter was now drawing a picture of his puppy, curled up asleep.

Mandy smiled. Timmy was *so* cute. She couldn't wait until home time, so she could see him again!

"Look, Peter, there they are!" Mandy said. She and Peter raced across the playground towards Mrs Foster and Timmy, who were waiting at the gates.

Mandy had enjoyed her first day in the Juniors. Miss Rushton had talked about all the new things they were going to do that term. But now it was time to play with Timmy!

"Hi, Mum, hi, Timmy!" Peter beamed as he took the pup and gave him a cuddle. "Did you miss me, boy?"

Mandy laughed. Timmy was bouncing up and down in Peter's arms and licking his owner's nose, with little yelps of delight. "Yes, I think he missed you!" she said. She scratched the top of Timmy's head. Timmy turned round and gave her a little lick too.

"Come on, let's go home,"
Mrs Foster said, smiling.

They set off down the street.
When they reached the corner,
Peter turned to Mandy.

"Would you like to carry
Timmy for a bit?" he asked.

"Oh, yes, please!" Mandy said.

Timmy snuggled down into
Mandy's arms. He seemed happy
to be carried, although he sat up
and had a good look when a
man with a German shepherd
dog went by.

"No, Timmy," Mandy told
him. "That dog's too big for you
to play with!"

"Ruff!" Timmy replied cheekily,

and licked Mandy's cheek.

When they got home, Peter and Mandy took Timmy into the living-room.

Mandy was hoping that Timmy would want to play. But the puppy ran behind the sofa, and didn't come back out.

"What are you doing, Timmy?" Peter said, bending down to take a look.

"That's his favourite place to sleep at the moment," Mrs Foster said, coming in from the kitchen. "He's been behind there all day."

Mandy knelt down at the other end of the sofa to look. "I don't think he's asleep," she said. "I think he's chewing something!"

"What!" Mrs Foster frowned, and quickly pulled the sofa away from the wall.

Timmy was having a lovely time chewing a very brightly-coloured and very soggy piece of material. He wagged his tail happily at everyone.

"Oh, no! That's your father's new tie, Peter!" Mrs Foster cried.

"Gran gave him that!" She tried
to grab the tie from Timmy, but
the puppy didn't want to let go.
He hung on grimly,
playing tug-o'-war.

On her hands and knees,
Mandy crept up on Timmy from
behind. She leaned over the pup
and gently prised the tie from his
tiny jaws.

Still playing, Timmy turned round and pounced on Mandy's lap. Mandy tried not to laugh. She held the tie out of Timmy's reach and handed it over to Mrs Foster.

Mandy thought it was the most awful tie she'd ever seen. It was bright green with purple and orange flowers all over it.

"Dad hates that tie!" Peter grinned at his mum. "And so do you!"

Mrs Foster laughed. "Yes, all right," she agreed. "But Timmy still shouldn't have chewed it."

They all looked at Timmy. He was tired out with all the excitement, and gave a big yawn. Then he lay down and curled up in a furry little ball, to go to sleep.

"Oh, Timmy!" Mrs Foster said, shaking her head. "That was *very* naughty!"

But Mandy saw that she was smiling.

Chapter Three

"Mum, Timmy's so cute!" Mandy said happily. "I can't wait for you to see him."

It was the next morning. Mrs Hope was taking Mandy to school today.

But when they arrived at the school gates, Mandy was very disappointed. Timmy, Peter and Mrs Foster were nowhere to be seen.

"Sorry, love," Mrs Hope said. "I must go, or I'll be late for my visit to Mrs Dawkins. One of her ponies is very poorly. I'll see Timmy another time, OK?"

"OK," Mandy said, waving goodbye as her mum drove off. Then she went into the playground and waited near the gate. Perhaps Peter was ill and wasn't coming to school today.

Then, just a few minutes before the bell, Mandy saw Peter and Mrs Foster rushing towards the gate. Peter's mum had Timmy in her arms.

"Oh, Mandy, guess what happened!" Peter panted. "Timmy chewed my dad's shoelaces so much, that when he went to put his shoes on, the laces fell to bits!"

"That's why we're so late," Mrs Foster explained. "We had to hunt around the house for another pair."

Timmy wagged his tail, not looking at all ashamed of himself.

"Oh, Timmy!" Mandy said.

"Mum, did I put my reading book in my bag?" Peter asked, trying to pull his rucksack off his back. "I can't remember."

"Let me look," Mrs Foster said. "Mandy, will you hold Timmy for me?"

Mandy nodded eagerly and took Timmy in her arms. Straight away, the puppy tried to chew Mandy's hair.

"No, Timmy," Mandy said, shaking her hair back out of the puppy's reach. "Dogs don't eat hair!"

Timmy gave a little bark, as if surprised to hear that. He turned his attention to the neck of Mandy's school sweatshirt, instead.

"Oh Timmy!" Mrs Foster sighed as she looked through Peter's rucksack. "Can't you *ever* stop chewing things?"

As Mandy gently pushed Timmy's mouth away from the neck of her sweatshirt, he started to chew her fingers. Mandy couldn't help laughing.

"Is my book there, Mum?" Peter asked anxiously. "Miss Rushton said we had to bring them back today."

"Yes, it's here," Mrs Foster replied, pulling the book out. "Oh no!"

Mandy, Peter and Mrs Foster stared at the book. One corner of it had been chewed, and there were tiny teethmarks on the glossy cover.

"I didn't notice that when I put it in my bag because I was in such a rush," Peter groaned. "Oh, Timmy!"

"Tell Miss Rushton we'll pay for it," Mrs Foster said, looking a bit annoyed now. "And Timmy, stop chewing Mandy's fingers!"

The bell rang, and Mandy  gave Timmy back to Peter's mum. She hoped that Mrs Foster wasn't *too* cross with Timmy.

Chapter Four

After assembly, Miss Rushton
showed Class 3 lots of pictures.
They talked about the people in
them. And then Miss Rushton
said, "Now I'd like to you write
about *your* home."

Mandy wrote about Animal
Ark and all the pets that visited
with their owners. Then she
leaned over to see what Peter had
written. He'd gone to sharpen his

pencil, but Mandy knew he wouldn't mind her looking . . .

I live in Church Lane with my mum and dad and my new puppy Timmy. His favourite things are sleeping and chewing. So far he's chewed Dad's new tie, Mum's purse, my pencil case, the bathmat, Dad's shoelaces and my reading book.

Mandy looked at Peter's pencil case. Sure enough, there were tiny teethmarks on the corner.

"It will be playtime in five minutes, Class 3," Miss Rushton called. "Try to finish your work."

Quickly Mandy picked up her pencil again, but she couldn't help feeling a bit worried. Timmy's chewing could get him into big trouble . . .

When they got into the playground a few minutes later, Peter said that he didn't feel like playing. Mandy offered him half her crisps, to cheer him up.

"Thanks," Peter said,
managing a small smile.

"Are you worried about Timmy
chewing things?" Mandy asked.

Peter nodded and looked
miserable. "Dad was cross about
his tie being chewed – and *really*
cross when his laces fell to pieces
this morning. But chewing is just
a game to Timmy," he said.

"We'll have to think of a less naughty game for him to play then," Mandy said. She put the empty crisp packet in the playground bin. Then she crossed her fingers for luck.

When the bell rang at the end of the day, Mandy and Peter hurried out into the playground. Mandy was going home with Peter again, for tea – and to play with Timmy, of course!

Peter's mum was waiting at the gate with Timmy in her arms. The puppy looked very pleased to see them. He barked a loud hello, his tail wagging madly.

"Have you been good today, Timmy?" Peter asked nervously, as he took the pup from his mum.

"He's been *very* good," Mrs Foster said, smiling, as they walked along.

Mandy and Peter sighed with relief.

"Good boy!" Mandy said, scratching Timmy's sweet little ears. Timmy wagged his tail harder and licked her hand.

"No, he hasn't chewed anything he shouldn't – because I had a really good idea," said Mrs Foster.

Mandy and Peter looked up at her, interested.

"You know those old red slippers that don't fit you any more, Peter?" Mrs Foster went on. "Well, I gave them to Timmy! I thought that if he had something of his own to chew, he might stop chewing everything else. And it seems to have worked!" she said.

"That's great, Mum!" said Peter happily.

They soon reached home.

"Right, I'll go and start cooking us some tea," Mrs Foster said.

Peter put Timmy down on the floor and he bounded off into the living-room.

He came back, carrying an old red slipper in his mouth. He showed it to Mandy, looking very pleased with himself.

"Oh, is that your new toy, Timmy? It's lovely!" Mandy said, laughing.

It certainly looked as if Mrs Foster's idea had done the trick!

Chapter Five

"I think we've tired Timmy out!"
Mandy grinned, as the little pup
gave a big yawn.

They'd been playing tug- o'-
war with Timmy and his slippers
for almost half an hour. But now
Timmy was stretched out on the
rug, his eyes closed and his head
between his paws.

"Tea's ready!" Peter's mum
called from the kitchen.

"You have a nice snooze, Timmy," Peter whispered.

He grinned at Mandy, and they both tiptoed out to the kitchen.

Mrs Foster had made fish fingers, chips and peas – and there was lemon drizzle cake and milk for afters.

Mandy ate as quickly as she could. She wanted to play with

Timmy again before her dad came to collect her.

Peter ate even more quickly than Mandy. "Let's go and see if Timmy's awake," he said, when he'd finished.

Mandy nodded eagerly. She crammed the last bite of cake into her mouth, then took her plate over to the sink. "Thanks, Mrs Foster," she said. "That was great!" Then she hurried after Peter.

In the living-room, one of Timmy's slippers lay on the rug and the other was behind an armchair. But there was no sign of Timmy.

"Timmy!" Peter called. "Where are you?"

Then, suddenly, there was a sound from upstairs.

"What's that noise?" Mrs Foster said, coming out of the kitchen. "Where's Timmy?"

Feeling very worried, Mandy quickly followed Peter and his mum upstairs. What was Timmy up to?

Timmy was lying on the landing, concentrating very hard. He was trying to get his tiny jaw around the heel of a shiny black shoe. The other black shoe lay nearby. And its toe was covered with tiny teethmarks . . .

Mandy's heart sank.

"Oh, *Timmy*!" Peter groaned. "Those are my new school shoes!"

"Timmy!" Mrs Foster gasped furiously. "Those shoes were very expensive! You bad dog!"

Timmy's ears went down, and he began to whimper. He knew he'd done something wrong.

Mandy felt so sorry for him.

"He didn't mean it, Mum," Peter said miserably, picking up his pet.

But Mrs Foster shook her head. "Bring Timmy downstairs, Peter," she snapped. "This is just too much!"

Now Mandy felt very worried. Timmy had gone too far this time, and Mrs Foster was *really* angry.

Chapter Six

Before Peter's mum could say anything else, the doorbell rang. It was Mandy's dad.

"Hello there, Mrs Foster," Mr Hope said, smiling. "I've come to take Mandy home—" Then he stopped as he saw how miserable everyone looked. "Is anything wrong?" he asked.

"Timmy's been very naughty," Mrs Foster said crossly.

"He's chewed Peter's school shoes – and they were brand new!"

"Well, I'm afraid that you can't stop puppies from chewing things," Mandy's dad said. "They need to chew, because they're teething – just like human babies! And sometimes they chew things they shouldn't."

"Mum gave Timmy my old slippers to chew, Mr Hope," said Peter. "And it stopped him chewing *some* other things . . . but then he went off and chewed my school shoes!"

Mandy looked anxiously at her dad. Would he be able to help Timmy?

"Well, it's not really Timmy's fault," said Mr Hope, calmly. "You see, he was given permission to chew your old slippers, Peter. Now Timmy thinks he can chew *anything* that smells the same, and he won't get told off."

"Oh!" Peter gasped. "I never thought of that."

"Oh, dear – then it's my
fault," said Mrs Foster. "It was my
idea to give Timmy the slippers."

Mr Hope looked at Peter and
Mandy. Then he smiled. "I think
we can sort this out quite easily.
Come on, you two. We're going
for a drive – and let's take
Timmy, too!"

Mr Hope drove out of Welford to the nearby town of Walton. He stopped outside the local pet shop, Piper's Pets.

"Your mum *was* right, Peter," Mr Hope said, as they all climbed out of the Land-rover. "Timmy does need his own things to chew. But they've got to be the right *kind* of things."

"You mean dog chews, Dad!" Mandy guessed.

Mr Hope nodded. "That's right, Mandy. Dog chews will help Timmy's teeth to be healthy and strong," he said, pushing open the pet shop door. "They're much better for him than slippers!"

Piper's Pets had lots of different dog chews to choose from. There were all sorts of colours, shapes and sizes. Timmy got very excited with all the interesting smells.

"These chews are perfect for Timmy," Mr Hope said, picking up some chunky sticks and some thin strips. "And they will taste a lot nicer to him than old slippers and new school shoes!"

"I think Timmy agrees with you, Mr Hope!" said Peter, grinning. Timmy was leaning over, trying to steal one of the chews from Mr Hope's hand.

"Make sure that you give Timmy lots of praise when he chews something he's supposed to, Peter," Mr Hope advised, as he paid for the chews.

Peter nodded. "I will. Thanks, Mr Hope!"

Mandy was glad to see that
Peter looked much happier.
Thank goodness her dad knew
what to do! She just hoped
Timmy would behave himself
from now on.

"Timmy's finished the chews
your dad bought him, Mandy,"
Peter said, a week later.

He and Mandy were in the
Fosters' living-room watching
TV. They had been playing
with Timmy, but now the
puppy was in
the kitchen,
eating his
supper.

"Timmy really loves them. But they only lasted a week!"

"Well, they stopped him from chewing things he shouldn't, didn't they?" Mandy asked.

Peter nodded. But before he could say anything else, there was a shout from the kitchen.

"Timmy!" Mrs Foster called. "Don't you dare!"

Peter and Mandy ran to the door. They were just in time to see Timmy dash through the open kitchen door and down the garden. He was trailing a blue and white tea towel behind him, like a flag.

"Timmy!" Mrs Foster yelled as she ran out of the kitchen after him. "Bring that back!"

"I think it's time to get Timmy some more chews!" Mandy grinned, as she and Peter ran to join in the chase.

Chapter One

"Mum, where do tigers live?" Mandy Hope asked. She was pasting a picture of a tiger into her animal scrapbook.

It was the first day of the half-term holiday, and almost time for morning surgery at Animal Ark. Mandy's mum and dad were vets. The surgery where they worked was built onto the back of their cottage.

Mandy loved that. There were always plenty of animals around!

Emily Hope looked up from the pile of letters she was opening. "Well, there are tigers in Russia, and some in China – but India has the most tigers," she said. "They like to live in the jungle."

Mandy stuck the picture down carefully on the next blank page. "I'd *love* to go to India and see the tigers!" she sighed.

Her mum smiled. "One day, we'll go," she promised. "Your scrapbook's getting very full. We'll buy a new one when we go shopping."

"Great!" Mandy said happily.

She had collected *loads* of pictures. She might even need *two* new scrapbooks!

"Mandy?"

Mandy looked round.

Jean Knox, the Animal Ark receptionist, had come into the kitchen.